Sunset Point

Sunset Point

A Shelter Bay Novel

JoAnn Ross

ISBN-10: 1941134114
ISBN-13: 9781941134115

New York Times bestselling author JoAnn Ross returns to Shelter Bay with a story of destiny, desire, danger, and a sea captain's ancient curse that's become local legend.

Someone to Watch Over Me

Independent, strong-willed Tess Lombardi has dedicated her life to fighting for justice. As a deputy district attorney, threats are merely part of the job. This time, with several high profile cases on the line, she reluctantly agrees to protection. Only to discover that Nate Breslin comes with his own risks. How can she trust a bodyguard who's stalked her? And lies for a living?

Former Marine sniper Nate Breslin has managed, at least most days, to leave danger and death in his past. Nate has his own reasons for tracking Tess down, but when her life is threatened, this mission becomes personal and he's willing to risk anything and everything to keep her safe.

As the danger escalates and her would-be killer closes in, Tess must learn to trust Nate. With her life. And her heart.

1

NATE BRESLIN HAD dreamed about her again last night. As always, she appeared in the midst of a violent thunderstorm, the black crepe of her mourning clothes swirling about her slender body in the cold, harsh wind. Without a word, she emerged from the tempest, gliding ever so slowly toward him, her hand outstretched as if reaching for his touch.

A gust of wind from the storm-tossed sea ruffled her black veil, and a sudden sulfurous flash of lightning illuminated her ghostly face. In response to the overwhelming sorrow in those lovely, soulful eyes, he held out his hand, offering whatever comfort he could.

She was closer now.

In another moment, their fingertips would touch.

Then, as always, dammit, she was gone.

•••

GIVING UP ON any more sleep for the night, Nate sat on the porch of his Shelter Bay home perched on the edge of a cliff and looked out over the waters of the Pacific Ocean. As he drank his coffee, he reassured himself—not for the first time—that the entire dream was nothing more than a figment of his imagination. Maybe even some weird PTSD thing he'd brought back from Iraq and Afghanistan.

He had, after all, seen a shitload of death. And rather than come home and try to forget it, Nate worked out his "issues," as the Marine shrink during his separation Transition Assistance Seminar had referred to them, by delving into the dark world of the supernatural.

He'd written his first novel after surviving Fallujah, the bloodiest battle of the Iraq War. His blog, which he'd mainly started to occupy himself during downtime, was part ground truth of war, part absurdities of military life, and part creative writing. It was his short story of gigantic camel spiders being sent out to eat enemy combatants that had gotten him noticed by the *New York Times*, which had signed him to write for their "At War" blog.

The camel story, based on an exaggerated myth of an actual carnivorous arachnid, which did not eat people or camels, fortuitously happened to be read by an editor at a New York publishing house, who'd offered him his first book contract while he was still deployed. A book that went on to win a Bram Stoker award for best first novel, stellar reviews, and the rest, as they say, was history.

Ghosts, vampires, werewolves, ghouls—these were merely his fictional stock-in-trade, nothing more. It was certainly not unusual for a story idea to come to him in the middle of the night.

On the other hand—and wasn't there always another hand?—Captain Angus MacGrath, his resident ghost, had turned out to be absolute fact. When the apparition had first appeared during the renovation of his rambling seaside home,

Nate had gone online and researched the house's history. A bit more digging disclosed that the captain had drowned below these same cliffs when his ship had gone down in a storm. Which was sort of weird since Nate's last book had been about a Bermuda Triangle area off this very same coast, into which a lot of ships had disappeared or been sunk. Including the one outside his window.

It had been after he'd moved in that the mystery woman had started appearing in his dreams. The logical explanation was that she was nothing more than a potential character lurking in the dark depths of his subconscious. Even as Nate assured himself that she was nothing more than an enticing product of his creative, often twisted mind, he didn't believe it.

Not when he could still see the anguish in those lovely dark eyes even when he was awake. Not when the evocative violet scent of her perfume lingered in the rose-tinged early-morning air. Not when he could vividly recall the tingling of his fingertips when their hands had come so heartbreakingly close to touching.

Not when his midnight visitor seemed so... real.

So alive.

Gazing down at the hulking metal skeleton of the capsized ship that MacGrath had been captaining when he'd drowned at sea, Nate decided that the time had come to stop dreaming of the woman and find out who the hell she was. And what she was so desperately trying to tell him.

2

THE MULTNOMAH COUNTY district attorney's office was in its usual state of chaos. The incessant clamor of phones was escalated by the hum of competing conversations. Cardboard cups, doughnut crumbs, and wrappers from fast-food takeout meals littered desktops. The atmosphere was laced with aggravation, frustration, stale coffee, and sweat.

Tess Lombardi loved it.

She'd never minded the breathless pace that her work as a deputy district attorney entailed. On the contrary, she thrived in the midst of what could only charitably be called bedlam.

The daughter of a Portland Police Bureau detective, she'd cut her teeth on the rarefied discipline of the law. When her parents had divorced a week before her tenth birthday, Mike Brown and Claudia Lombardi nad agreed that it would be best if Tess remained with her father. No one concerned had ever regretted that decision.

Claudia was free to travel the world like a beautiful, jet set social butterfly, unencumbered by a growing child. While Mike, unlike so many of his divorced friends on the force, was able to keep his daughter under both his wing and his roof.

When Tess was twelve—despite the Lombardi custom that all the women maintained their family surname—she'd announced to her father that she wanted to go to court and change her last name to his. Which was when Mike Brown had assured her that he'd always love her, whatever her name. But he also wanted her to never forget that her mother's wine-growing family could trace its direct lineage to the Lombard conquest of Tuscany in the sixth century. Having arrived from Italy in the 1800s, the Willamette Valley Lombardis had become one of the first families to commercially grow grapes.

But Mike was the son of a drug dealer who'd been killed in prison and an alcoholic mother who'd often forget she'd left her infant alone at home. He'd landed in foster care before his first birthday, had been moved to a group home for wayward and homeless boys at age three, and then self-emancipated at sixteen. Appreciating the importance of roots, he'd encouraged Tess to recognize and embrace her own.

As usual, her father's instincts had been right. While she might not carry his last name, the big, outwardly tough man with the warm and soft heart had been everything a father could be. His unreserved love had provided all the nurturing and encouragement any young girl could ever need.

Tess's fondest memories were of the times she was allowed to watch him testify in court. Detective Michael Xavier Brown of the Portland Police Bureau was more than her father. He was her superhero—Superman, Batman, and the X-Men all rolled into one husky, gregarious human being. Although she'd attended law school rather than follow him into the department, Tess never entered a courtroom without thinking how she was continuing her father's life work to gain justice for those unable to achieve it for themselves.

As she returned to her office to pick up some papers after court this afternoon, however, Tess was more than a little irritated to be running behind schedule.

When she tossed her briefcase down, the woman at the neighboring desk glanced up in surprise. "I didn't expect you back. Aren't you due in Shelter Bay by five?"

"Five thirty," Tess said. "Of all days for Larry Parker to play Perry Mason, he had to pick this one. You should have seen him on defense this morning. I could not believe one man, especially one with such a limited vocabulary, could be so long-winded.

"By the time Judge Keane declared a lunch recess, we were already running forty-five minutes late. Fortunately, the judge must've had a hot date, because he cut off testimony and sent everyone home early."

It hadn't escaped anyone's notice that ever since *Portland Monthly* magazine had named Judge Gerald Keane the city's most eligible bachelor, early adjournments were happening more and more often.

"The boost to his social life appears to have shortened the court day," Alexis Montgomery agreed. "But there's also the fact that ever since he decided to run for that vacant seat on the Court of Appeals, the judge hasn't passed up an opportunity to make a speech. I read that he was talking to the Business Alliance at a cocktail mixer at the downtown Marriott this evening."

"Finally," Tess said. "A reason to be grateful for politics. If I'd had to listen to Larry another five minutes, I'd have started slamming my head onto the desk."

"If you're driving down to Shelter Bay, it can only mean that Dana White is getting cold feet about testifying."

"She's apprehensive," Tess admitted. "But I can certainly understand her feelings. What woman would want to admit to the world that she married a man who already had twenty wives scattered throughout fifteen states?"

"Well, I wouldn't worry too much about the Shelter Bay Mrs. Schiff if I were you. Fortunately, there are enough women out there who want to see the guy drawn and quartered that we shouldn't have any trouble getting a conviction. Especially with the case Donovan handed us all tied up with that pretty red ribbon."

Donovan Quinn was a detective in the Portland Police Bureau who'd tirelessly worked the bigamist case from the beginning, tracking down all the loose ends to make that pretty bow. Like all the cases he brought to the D.A.'s office, the investigation had been impeccable, making him a prosecutor's dream detective. Having dated him a few times before they'd decided to remain friends, Tess also knew him to be one of the good guys.

"I know we don't need her," Tess agreed. "But I have the feeling Dana needs us. Her self-confidence has taken a big hit, and she sounded shaky the last time I talked with her on the phone."

Alexis leaned back in her chair. "Sometimes I think you're too softhearted to be in this business, Lombardi."

"Why don't you try telling that to the much-married Melvin Schiff?" Tess countered. "One of the reporters down at the courthouse couldn't wait to show me today's *Oregonian*."

"That bad, huh?"

"Schiff was quoted as saying that I was such an icy bitch that if any man even was willing to have sex with me, his penis would freeze off."

"Shut up. They did not write that."

"No, they put in an asterisk for the *i* in bitch and went with a *'certain part of the anatomy'* for penis, which, I suspect, is still a more polite term than he actually used."

"The guy's a real charmer."

"Isn't he? I can't figure out what all those women saw in him."

"He's a con man," Alexis said. "I suppose, looking at the big picture, we—and all those women who fell for his slimy grifter ways—ought to be grateful he isn't some sociopath who kills his wives for their insurance money. His M.O. was to do a juggling act between families for as long as he could get away with it, clean out the bank accounts, then move on."

"Leaving them alive but devastated," Tess said. "And speaking of moving on, I'd better get going. As it is, I'm probably going to have to break every speeding law on the books to get there in time."

"At least if you get stopped, you can argue your own case. Want some company?"

Tess considered the offer for a moment, then shook her head. "I don't think so. You've been working around the clock on that arson case the past three weeks. Besides, aren't you going out with Matt tonight?"

"I could cancel. It's not as if he isn't used to it."

Which was life as normal in the D.A.'s office. Tess couldn't remember the last time she'd had a date. Nor a day off, including weekends. There were even times when she thought that if her townhouse ever became a crime scene, one look at the contents of her refrigerator and cupboards would have investigators questioning whether anyone actually lived there.

"You just happen to be engaged to the man voted Portland's second sexiest bachelor," she reminded her best friend. "And we both know he only lost first place to the judge because you guys got engaged, which took him off the market. Besides, after the hours you've been putting in, you both deserve to get lucky."

Alexis grinned. "Now that you mention it, although I meant my offer to go along to Shelter Bay for moral support, that's pretty much what I was planning when I went shopping at lunch." She reached beneath her desk and pulled out a shopping bag from Portland's premiere French lingerie boutique.

"Ooh la la." Tess lifted an ebony brow. "You're pulling out the heavy weaponry."

"You bet I am. In this designer bag, I happen to have a bustier, garter belt and hand-dyed vintage stockings designed to knock Matt's socks off...along with the rest of his clothes."

"If you weren't my best friend, I'd have to hate you," Tess, whose only sex life for too long had involved batteries, complained. She was still laughing as she left the office, headed down the hall.

Another deputy district attorney was headed her way, his expression that of a depressed bloodhound. "Hey, Tess," he greeted her with a poor attempt at a smile. "Heard what your bigamist said. Which should make it even more satisfying when you take him down."

"How did you know about me liking this place?" she asked after they'd ordered drinks—a craft beer for him, ice water with a slice of lemon for her.

"I have a spy in your camp," he admitted.

"A spy?"

"Alexis Montgomery."

That was the most surprising thing the man had said thus far. And even more difficult to accept than his stupid alleged ghost.

"I don't believe you. Alexis is my best friend. She'd never give away my secrets."

His mouth quirked at the corner. "The fact that you enjoy one of the city's more popular dining spots is not exactly a sacred trust, Ms. Lombardi."

Objection overruled. She chalked up a point for him. "So what else did Alexis tell you? And how do you know her?"

The server chose that moment to arrive with their drinks, then took their meal order, making her wait for his response until they were alone again.

"Matt Miller is my attorney. And except for the information that you're a dynamite prosecutor who just happens to appreciate farm-to-table food, as well as telling me that you are much too good for me, Alexis didn't reveal a single, solitary personal thing about you, Tess."

As he took a drink of his beer, Nate saw the relief in her eyes. Alexis was right, he mused. Tess Lombardi was an intensely private person. As was he. Nate liked the idea that they had something in common besides fresh food. And the captain.

"You really were terrific this morning," he said, his smile coaxing one in return. "I guarantee that the jury will come in with a unanimous decision for conviction."

"I'd like to think you're right. But the day I believe I can read a jury is the day I chuck law and head for Las Vegas and become a professional poker player."

"Let me know so I can get my bets down," he said with an easygoing grin meant to encourage her to relax.

"You'll be the first to know," she said as the server returned to the table with their lunches. She picked up her fork and took a bite of her field greens salad. "This is delicious." And an admitted treat given that, like everyone else in the office, she usually ate her lunch at her desk. No one ever became a government prosecutor for the salary or lifestyle.

"Lombardi," he murmured thoughtfully as he cut into his pulled pork sandwich. "I put a great deal of my royalties into the coffers of Lombardi Wineries. I don't suppose you happen to be—"

"Luca Lombardi was my four-times-great-grandfather," Tess cut in. "He started the winery with vines he brought over from his family's vineyard in Tuscany."

The name instantly rang a bell. *Damn.* No wonder she'd stiffened when he'd brought the subject up. Nate had just graduated middle school when eight-year-old Tess Lombardi had disappeared while walking back to the Lombardis' vast estate, where she'd been visiting her maternal grandmother. Twenty-four hours later, her mother, Claudia Lombardi, had received a ransom note demanding a million dollars in uncut diamonds for her child's safe return.

The family had paid the ransom, Nate recalled. Although the news hadn't been 24/7 back in those days, it was impossible to miss talk of the frightening case of the kidnapped young heiress. Even as far away as Orchid Island, where he'd grown up. Although he'd never admit it to her, the event had inspired a short story for a writing competition. But in his version, her character had been beamed up into a spaceship by aliens.

As updates of the case turned up on the nightly news every night, his mother and father, and those of every other kid he knew, had suddenly turned hypervigilant, making today's helicopter parents seem downright laid-back by comparison.

It was two more desperate weeks before the sheriff and her dad had found her in what was essentially a hidey-hole at a remote cabin in the coastal mountains. Although a medical examination had declared her physically unharmed, the press had openly speculated about the child's emotional health for weeks.

Six months later her father Mike Brown, a Portland police detective, had tracked the Lombardi housekeeper—who'd disappeared the day of the kidnapping—to Idaho. In a stroke of unfortunate timing, he'd arrived hours after the woman's death, which a coroner had ruled to be a suicide. Although never proven, there were those, including Brown, who believed that the woman had been murdered by someone wanting to ensure she'd never talk about the crime.

"I'm sorry. Now I understand why you reacted so harshly when I grabbed you. Which I apologize for. Even without your history, that was out of bounds. And, honestly, way out of character for me." His deep voice softened with sympathy. "It must have brought back a lot of memories."

"That's where you're wrong." There'd been times when Tess couldn't decide whether her lack of memory of the experience was a good or bad outcome.

"Yet I frightened you."

"Of course you did. It was getting dark, I was alone, and you were a much-larger strange man who came out of the shadows and grabbed me. Any woman in her right mind would have been scared."

"I can't argue with that," he said. "But I still believe we're talking more than expected nerves."

Those clear, intelligent eyes saw too much. In that respect, he reminded her of Donovan. "All right. I'll admit it. I was scared." The control she'd demonstrated in the courtroom slipped a bit as her fingers tightened on her fork. "I've been receiving some calls that have made me uncharacteristically jumpy. My first thought was that you might be him."

"Damn. Now I'm really sorry. What kind of calls?"

"Merely the anonymous kind that come with the job. And I have absolutely no idea why I'm telling you this."

The only other people who knew about the calls were Donovan Quinn, Multnomah County District Attorney Thomas Barnes, Jake, and Alexis. Tess hadn't even told her father.

Despite having retired from the force after a heart attack six months ago, Mike Brown wouldn't hesitate to track down any bad guy who might dare threaten his daughter. Something she refused to risk for fear of causing another attack.

"Perhaps you're telling me because of this." Nate reached into his pocket, pulled out a piece of paper, and handed it to her.

"It's a surprisingly good likeness," she murmured, studying the extremely flattering sketch. "You didn't mention you're also an artist."

"I'm not. I can't paint anything but a wall, but I did inherit an amateuristic ability to sketch from my mother, who's a professional artist. My father paints, too, but only as a hobby."

"This is a step up from amateur work," she said. "But it's a little presumptuous of you to change my hairstyle."

"I didn't change it."

She looked up at him. "Of course you did. You drew me with straight hair. My curls have driven me crazy for years."

He waved away her argument. "Your curls are gorgeous. But I couldn't have known the difference in the hairstyles when I drew that sketch."

"When did you draw it?"

"Eight weeks ago."

"That's ridiculous, we—"

"Hadn't met yet." Nate's gaze was unnerving as it swept over her face.

"You could have seen me on TV. My bigamist case has gotten a lot of coverage."

"I don't watch the news, especially when I'm on a deadline, which is almost always. There's too much bad stuff on it."

"Says the man who writes about even worse things."

"My books are fiction. I did look you up after I found your wallet. Google kicked up a lot of pages about the money-laundering trials. Obviously I didn't read deeply enough to get to your past."

"It's encouraging to learn that my work shows up before that old kidnapping story."

"It does. And it's all good. Including an article that suggested you were considering running for congress."

"Now *that's* definitely fiction."

"Too bad. The political system, which has become a horror story of its own, could use someone like you...And I'm betting you really don't believe in ghosts."

Tess took a soothing sip of ice water. What he was suggesting was not only ludicrous, it was impossible. She couldn't help wondering if all those years of writing about monsters had affected the man's mind.

"No, I don't. And for the record, nor do I believe in vampires, sparkly or otherwise, werewolves, ghouls, or any other spooky things that go bump in the night." Tess speared a piece of romaine topped with pomegranate seeds. "With such a vivid imagination, it's no wonder your books sell so well."

"That sketch isn't a figment of my imagination. And believe me, Tess, neither is Captain MacGrath."

Tess froze at the all-too-familiar name.

Busted. Nate had sensed there were hidden depths to Tess Lombardi. Angus MacGrath might be a clever old soul, but he couldn't have captured Nate's unwavering interest with just any woman.

"I suspect most people who've visited Shelter Bay have heard the name." After taking another drink of ice water, she drew in a deep, calming breath. "Given that the wreck of the ship he was captaining is still rusting away on Castaway Cove."

Every instinct Nate possessed told him that Tess knew more than she was telling, but before he could dig deeper, they ran out of time.

She put down her glass and stood up. "I'm due back in court to make my closing statement."

Nate tossed some bills on the table. "Don't worry, Counselor, I'll get you back before the bailiff calls the court to order."

The sun was shining through a break in the slate-gray clouds as they left the restaurant.

"We didn't get to finish our conversation," he said as they walked back to the courthouse. "Have dinner with me tonight."

"So I can waste my time listening to you drag out this outrageous bit of fiction concerning the alleged ghost of a man who died a century ago?"

"I can see that your work would make you cynical," Nate allowed. "And granted, it does sound like an outrageous story. But it's not fiction."

"I don't know what game it is you're playing here, Mr. Breslin—"

"It's Nate," he reminded her. "We shared a lunch, which you didn't finish. And you can deny it until doomsday, but we're also somehow personally connected through the captain. I'd say that allows you to call me by my first name."

"I don't *want* any connection with you, personal or otherwise."

"Hey." He held up both hands as they reached the steps of the courthouse. "I didn't ask the guy to put you in my dreams, okay? I'm just trying to figure out why."

"If he has done that—and I'm not admitting for a moment that I believe your crazy claim about his existence to be true—it's not me who's been appearing in your dreams."

Nate's right brow rose in an unmistakable sign of irritation. "I suppose you have a better explanation for that sketch? A drawing I did before I'd ever met you?"

"I can't explain what possessed you to draw it in the first place," Tess admitted reluctantly.

"Now we're getting somewhere. So you're willing to admit that some indefinable force is responsible?"

"No." Tess shook her head. "As I said, I've no idea why you drew it. But whatever the reason, you're way off base."

"What's that supposed to mean?"

"*You're* the one with the vivid imagination," she tossed back as she started up the stone steps of the courthouse. "You figure it out."

Nate frowned, not wanting to let her get away quite yet but knowing he had no choice. How cooperative would Tess be if he made her late for court? Not very. In fact, considering how seriously she took her work, she'd probably never speak to him again.

But, dammit, he'd been right. She knew. Somehow, in some unfathomable way, he and Tess Lombardi were mysteriously linked. And the captain, as he had suspected all along, was the key.

Just as he was trying to figure out his next move, Tess appeared to take pity on him.

"The sketch is of my great-great-grandmother," she informed him over her shoulder. "So if your dreams *have* honestly been haunted by a Lombardi, it's Isabella, not me."

As she turned away again, Nate watched her with a mixture of lingering irritation and masculine appreciation. She might act like the Marine drill sergeant he'd suffered under for all those weeks of basic training after he graduated from college, but Tess Lombardi had the best legs of any woman he'd ever met.

"You may think you've had the last word, Counselor," he murmured. "But believe me, lady, we've only just begun."

Nate was smiling as he left Portland and drove back to Shelter Bay. Tess might have been right when she'd suggested it was her ancestor who'd been playing a starring role in his dreams night after night.

But now that he'd met Isabella's intriguing great-great-granddaughter, if the woman thought he was going to simply write the entire experience off as a case of mistaken identity, she wasn't nearly as intelligent as he'd already determined her to be.

Oh, no. He and Tess Lombardi weren't finished yet, Nate vowed.

Not by a long shot.

12

"TRAITOR."

Alexis glanced up at Tess, her expression giving nothing away. "I heard things went well in court today. Congratulations."

Tess leaned forward, resting her hands on the surface of her friend's desk. "You conspired with Nate Breslin to trick me into lunch."

"Ah. I take it he caught up with you?"

"He did," Tess muttered.

"You don't sound particularly pleased. You can't tell me the food wasn't great."

"The food was excellent, as always. It was the company that left a great deal to be desired."

Alexis began straightening the correspondence in her out basket. "That's odd," she murmured. "Nate is usually a fascinating conversationalist."

"I suppose he might seem that way. To someone who finds ghouls and goblins fascinating."

"Nate is a little bent," Alexis admitted. "But I've always thought that was one of the most appealing things about him. It's fascinating to watch him think his way around corners."

Picking up a rubber band, she put it away in a drawer. "Of course, his gorgeous gemstone-green bedroom eyes aren't so bad, either."

"What are you doing noticing his eyes? You're engaged."

"I'm engaged, not dead." Her expression sobered. "You know, he's very nice."

"Oh, really?" Tess replied with feigned disinterest. "Personally, I found him tiring." She shook her head. "Besides, his behavior could only be classified as bizarre. He actually spent the entire lunch telling me a ghost story."

"I've always enjoyed Nate's stories," Alexis countered easily. She took a drink of coffee from the ever-present mug on her desk. "You know, there's something to be said against being too choosy."

"That's easy for you to say. After all, you just happen to be engaged to one of the smartest, as well as nicest, men I've ever met. Not to mention him being super hot."

"Matthew and Nate are the opposite sides of a very attractive coin," Alexis agreed. "And I hadn't realized you'd taken such notice of my fiancé's attributes." Alexis's smile was calm and confident.

"I'm choosy, not dead."

The women shared a laugh before returning to their work. After ten minutes, Tess looked up from the lengthy transcript of the Kagan case.

"Alexis?"

"Mmm?" The other woman was lost in a law book, taking notes on a yellow legal pad.

"Do you...Well, have you ever...Oh, skip it," she said as she twisted a paper clip into figure eights. "The entire thing's absolutely ridiculous."

Her atypical uneasiness had captured Alexis's attention. "What's ridiculous?"

Tess shook her head. "Never mind. It's not important."

Alexis put down her pen and waited.

"Do you believe in ghosts?" Tess asked.

Alexis took her time in answering. "No," she said at length. "I don't believe I do, although I can't deny that I find the idea intriguing. Do you?" she asked. "Believe?"

"Of course not," Tess insisted, not entirely truthfully as she tossed away the mangled paperclip. "Forget it. I'm sorry I brought it up."

Alexis continued to observe her for another long moment. "Sure," she said finally, returning to her research. "Consider it forgotten."

Nate Breslin's ludicrous story about a ghost living in his house had to be a fabrication. There wasn't any ghost of Captain Angus MacGrath because ghosts didn't exist. They couldn't. The entire idea of some lost soul, trapped between his earthly existence and some ethereal paradise, was nothing but a fantasy created by novelists and screenwriters.

Tess told herself that over and over as she drove home at the end of the day. She reminded herself continually of the fact as she turned on every light in her townhouse before fixing a bowl of cereal for dinner.

"I don't believe this," she moaned later as she turned her television to the Classic Film Channel. She had intended to put Nate Breslin and his ridiculously tall tale out of her mind by losing herself in an old movie, only to discover that tonight's offering was none other than *The Ghost and Mrs. Muir.*

"There are no such things as ghosts," she said aloud, aiming the remote control at the television just as Rex Harrison, playing the spirit of an ancient seaman, appeared in the kitchen of Gull Cottage. The screen went dark. "They're nothing more than fictional characters. Or figments of nervous minds," she added as the wind coming off the river began to howl eerily down her chimney.

Settling down with a romance novel, Tess vowed to put both the annoying horror writer and his ghostly friend from her mind. But despite her best efforts, she still jumped when a shutter on an upstairs window suddenly banged.

"There are no such things as ghosts," she repeated determinedly, picking up the book she'd dropped onto the rug. The flames of the gas fire she'd turned on to warm up a rainy night were creating tall, flickering shadows on the wall. "It's ridiculous to even be thinking about one."

As she struggled to ignore the wind's lonely wail, Tess felt like a little girl whistling past a graveyard.

13

T ESS WOKE THE following morning with a splitting head-
ache and the unsettling feeling that she'd spent the night
in another dimension. She'd had a dream. A dream of her kidnapping so vivid that she'd awakened time after time unable
to discern what was real and what was only the product of an
overworked, over-stimulated subconscious.

She'd been in the dark. Curled up on a rough woolen
blanket that scratched her skin and smelled like a wet dog.
She'd lost track of the time and would have been unable to
tell if it were day or night if it weren't for the masked man
occasionally bringing her food and water.

An Egg McMuffin was breakfast, which told her she'd sur-
vived another night. Chicken McNuggets were another marker,
letting her know that a day had gone by and she was still alive.

But how many days? Time had blurred.

She'd heard the squeak of floorboards overhead. Seen a
rectangle of light as the hidden doorway opened. Then iden-
tified the sound of heavy boots pounding down the stairs.

It was a familiar nightmare. One she'd had at least weekly
into her teens, then it had, for several years, suddenly gone

away. Until recently, when it had returned from where it had been lurking in the far, darkest reaches of her mind.

Unfortunately, or perhaps fortunately, she always woke up before discovering to whom those boots belonged. But because she knew the outcome of the story, she'd always believed it had been her dad and imagined him scooping her up into his strong arms and holding her against his chest, the way he must have held her when she was a baby.

Did she remember or imagine the tears streaming down her face?

And if they'd been real, had they been her father's? Or hers? Or both?

Not doing anything to ease her unrelenting stress, she'd also received another threat from her anonymous caller sometime in the middle of the night. This time he'd accused her of putting an innocent man in prison and suggested that she watch her step very, very carefully.

Her head was still pounding when she reached the office, where she poured a paper cupful of water from the cooler and tossed down her third Advil of the morning.

"Rough night?" Alexis asked sympathetically, handing her a cup of black coffee and a chocolate-frosted donut from a box someone had brought in.

"Thanks," Tess said. "I just had too much spinning around in my head to get much sleep." Even as she vowed to run after work to avoid the donut attaching itself directly to her hips, no way could she resist the aroma of warm fried fat and chocolate.

"If you'd gone out to dinner with Nate, your night might have turned out a lot better."

Despite her friend's quasi-denial of matchmaking, Tess still believed that Alexis had hoped the lunch would lead to something else.

Like matching rings, picket fences, and strollers. None of which Tess was interested in. She wasn't saying *never*. Just not now. And especially not with a man who was either delusional or a liar.

"Don't tell me that Matt is so desperate for work that he'd try to marry Nate off just for the opportunity to update his will and write a prenup."

"Did I mention anything about marriage? For the sake of our friendship, I'll ignore the snark," Alexis declared haughtily. "Besides, for your information, Matthew just happens to agree with me."

"About what?"

"That, first of all, you are far too much of a workaholic who needs to get out more. When was the last time you took a long, romantic walk along the river? When did you stop to enjoy the feel of the breeze in your hair, the scent of flowers at the Japanese Gardens, a dazzling sunset—"

"I get the idea," Tess broke in dryly. "I just can't tell if you're describing a shampoo commercial or one for a little blue erectile dysfunction pill. But while we're on the topic of Matthew, what else does your paragon of a fiancé agree with you about?"

"We agree most of the time," Alexis said. "Sometimes it's almost boring how alike we are. But in this case, we both think that you and Nate would make an ideal couple."

Tess sputtered out a laugh. "You've got to be kidding. The man and I are light-years apart. We have absolutely nothing in common." Except, admittedly, their choice in restaurants. Which didn't mean anything. After all, the reason for the restaurant's longevity was that it was a favorite of lots of Portlanders. That didn't mean she was destined to marry any of them.

There was also the fact that Breslin and she did, in a few degrees of separation way, have Captain MacGrath in common, Tess allowed. Enough that he'd somehow also infiltrated her dreams last night. But sometime during the predawn hours, she'd vowed to stop thinking about her errant, long-dead great-great-grandfather.

"Hey Tess." Their conversation was interrupted by a tall, sandy-haired man sporting an unfortunate comb-over, who stopped by Tess's desk on his way to the coffee bar. "I hear Vasilyev's lawyer's going after a federal habeas corpus ruling."

Grigori "The Viper" Vasilyev was one of Tess's more successful cases. Since it was also her first case when she'd joined the district attorney's office, she'd been assigned to Jim Stevens, a veteran prosecutor. Although the Russian mobster had used the U.S. justice system for all it was worth, winning delay after delay, both Jim and Tess had remained adamant that the man should stand trial, and eventually he had, drawing a life-plus-twenty-year sentence for drugs, murder, conspiracy to commit murder, criminal assault, illegal gambling, and human trafficking.

After having lost his appeal on the judgment of conviction, and two years later another loss on a post-conviction appeal, his last-ditch attempt to claim that his constitutional rights had been violated in the Oregon court system because the infirmary hadn't had a Russian-speaking doctor on staff when he'd suddenly come down with shortness of breath, rapid heartbeat, and chest pain (which had not proven to be a heart attack) didn't surprise her.

"He'll lose again. Just as he always does. Because he's guilty as sin."

And also because she had a witness willing to testify that not only was Vasilyev continuing to run his empire while in prison, he'd purposely injected himself with an overdose of anabolic steroids to cause the symptoms that would land him in the infirmary in the first place. Given that his English was as good as hers, Tess knew he'd gone through all that subterfuge in order to claim federal discrimination for anti-nationality reasons.

Granted, Vasilyev's attorney would paint her informant to be a jailhouse snitch, which, indeed, he was. The low-level dealer to the prison gym rats was also hoping to cut a deal that would expunge infractions that had added more time to his sentence.

Adding yet another dark mark against him, he'd been the one who'd been selling the bulked-up Russian the illegal steroids in the first place.

But Tess had driven to the penitentiary in Salem herself, and while her work had admittedly made her cynical, she'd believed the informer who'd told her that The Viper was plotting yet another murder while inside those brick walls.

"Maybe so." Bill Mitchell snagged a maple-glazed Long John from the bakery box. "But I sure as hell admire your guts. If I had your connections and mucho wine bucks, I'd blow this pop stand, buy myself my own tropical island, and live la dolce vita."

"I have a job."

"One that probably doesn't cover your shoe budget."

Since when was appreciating a well-made, beautiful shoe a crime? "I'd rather work than spend my spare time drinking mai tais and polishing seashells," she said, deciding not to share that escape to exactly such a place was on her to-do list.

"You could always work for your family's winery."

"I don't know anything about running a vineyard. All I do is cosign the checks. Besides," she added, "the only interest I have in wine is drinking it. I love my job here."

"Even when it makes enemies of guys like Vasilyev?"

"We're already enemies. That was decided when I chose to prosecute criminals and Vasilyev chose to *be* one. Besides, he threatened to have me killed the day of his sentencing, and as you can see, I'm certainly still around."

"But your former mentor and co-counsel on that case isn't," Mitchell pointed out.

A cold shiver skimmed up Tess's spine. "That was an accident," she insisted, citing the Coast Guard's findings.

She didn't mention that her recent calls coming so soon after her co-prosecutor's death three months ago was—along with the murder of the Salem deputy district attorney who'd prosecuted another one of the Russian's gang—the reason the police had gotten a warrant to listen in on her phone calls. "Accidents happen. Even to the best of sailors." Which Jim Stevens had definitely been.

"Hey," Alexis broke in, "can't you two discuss something a little more cheerful? At least until I've had my second cup of coffee?"

Mitchell grinned sheepishly and held up both hands. "Sorry." He turned his attention back to Tess. "I still think you've got major cojones. For a girl," he said before continuing across the room.

Tess and Alexis watched him go. "He meant that as a compliment. I think," Alexis said finally.

Tess sighed. "I know. It's just that I really don't like him." She shook her head, watching as he stopped yet again to joke with another prosecutor. "He's rude, sexist, and totally lacking in tact." He was also slick. No, that wasn't exactly it. More *slimy*. If he were a mobster, his name would be Bill "The Slug" Mitchell.

"Speaking of your taste in men," Alexis said, smoothly turning the conversation back to its original track, "I promise not to mention it again, but I still contend that you and Nate could work out." Her friend's eyes had the gleam of an unrepentant matchmaker.

"Really," she insisted when Tess rolled her eyes. "You don't believe anything unless you read it in the *The Oregonian* in black and white. Despite his Marine years at war, including being wounded in an IED explosion, which should have made him cynical, Nate tends to believe in everything until he's proven wrong." Alexis's smile was guileless. "See?"

"The only thing I see is that somehow, when I wasn't looking, you've turned into one of those women who, just because you've found happiness with a man, wants to send every woman up a white satin aisle for a life of wedded bliss."

"Would that be so bad?"

Tess rose abruptly from her desk, brushing scattered doughnut crumbs off her fog-gray pencil skirt. "I don't believe in marriage."

"Ah, yes," Alexis drawled. "How foolish of me. I'd almost forgotten the infamous Lombardi curse."

"You can laugh all you want." Tess picked up her briefcase, checking to be sure she had everything she needed for a long day in court. "But the fact remains that no Lombardi woman, from Isabella on, has managed to live happily ever after, including me. Captain MacGrath, bastard that he was, saw to that."

"How in the world can you continue to insist that you and Nate aren't a match made in heaven when you say things like that?" Alexis argued doggedly. "He's one of the few people I know on this earth who might actually buy that outlandish tale of the captain's curse."

Tess knew Alexis was right. She also knew it was totally uncharacteristic of her to give the story, which had become legend in the Lombardi family, any credence. But try as she might to discount it, she couldn't deny that, beginning with her great-great-grandmother Isabella, every single one of the Lombardi women had proven disastrously unlucky in love.

"Look," she said. "I'm happy for you and Matt. Truly I am. And if I ever run across a man as perfect for me as he is for you, I might even take another chance on reaching for that brass ring. But believe me, Nate Breslin is not that man."

"That's your opinion, but you haven't even given yourself a chance to get to know him yet."

"I don't want to get to know him. Besides, when it comes to my love life, my opinion is the only one that matters." Giving her friend a warning look, Tess turned to leave the office.

"I'm still putting my money on Nate," Alexis said. "In fact, I'm looking forward to watching him wear down your resistance."

"Don't bother; you'd only be wasting your time. Now if we're through discussing my love life..."

"Or lack of," Alexis got in the final word as Tess walked away.

• • •

As she left the courtroom at the end of her day, Tess found Nate waiting for her again.

"You were brilliant," he told her. "If I were the D.A., I'd be worried about my job."

Tess shook her head. "I'd never want to be district attorney. The profile's too high."

"And we've already determined that you're a lady who protects her privacy."

Tess nodded. "Got it. And as much as I'd love to stand here and chat, I have to get back to my office."

Why was she not surprised he had no intention of letting her get away that easily? "How about having dinner with me when you get off?"

"I'm sorry, but I have plans." She didn't add that she intended to spend the evening wading through mountains of depositions in preparation for the Schiff case.

"Why do I get the feeling that you'd have plans for whatever evening I suggested?"

"Probably because, while you may be mentally disturbed, you're perceptive," she answered without missing a beat.

"Why don't you try humoring me?"

"What did you think I was doing yesterday?"

"Having lunch with a man who hasn't been able to get you out of his mind." He crossed his ankles, leaned against the wall, folded his arms, and looked down at her.

25

"NATE BRESLIN SEEMS like a nice enough man," Eleanor said as Mike drove her home.

"He doesn't have a record, and the people Jake talked to in Shelter Bay only had positive things to say about him."

"You had him investigated?"

"As soon as Jake ran his plates. I *am* an investigator," he reminded her. "That's what I do."

When she folded her arms, he felt a chill come over the inside of the car. "Can I expect to have you look into my life?"

"Of course not. Unless," he tacked on after a moment's pause, "you started getting threatening calls or someone tried to hurt you. Then I'd be on the case like white on rice."

"Because that's what you do."

"No. Because I like you."

"You barely know me."

"Cops have good instincts. And you have dynamite legs."

He liked that she laughed. "I like you, too. And not because you have great guns."

"You're not talking about my service Glock."

"No." She reached out and curled her fingers around his upper arm. "I'm talking about the fact that you obviously keep in good shape."

"I work out some."

Despite what the TV shows and movies suggested, cops and detectives spent more time sitting on their asses than they did chasing bad guys. Not wanting to look like a stereotypical Dunkin' Donuts cop, he'd always passed his annual physical with flying colors.

"I do, too. But, while I endure the stairstepper and treadmill, I much prefer yoga."

Mike knew he was in deep, deep trouble when an image of Eleanor in those clingy workout clothes women wore doing a downward dog or whatever those twisty movements were made him as instantly hard as he'd been at sixteen.

Which, in turn, had him grateful for two things: that it was dark in the car, and he wouldn't be needing blue pills if she decided one day to take their relationship to the next level.

"Getting back to your daughter and the novelist, I doubt she'd be happy to know you've been checking up on her."

"She'd be pissed," Mike allowed. "But she'd get over it. Because she knows I love her and want to protect her." Which, dammit, he hadn't always been able to do. And didn't memories of that time still feel like a stone in the gut?

"Do you always investigate men she's involved with?"

"No." If he had, he would've realized she'd married one of those cops who crossed the line when it came to control issues. "Just the ones who threaten her."

The slight hint of disapproval he'd heard in her tone turned to surprise. "I have a hard time imagining that young man threatening anyone."

"He's a Marine," Mike pointed out. "Who's done multiple tours in Iraq and Afghanistan. Which means he's tougher than he looks, and could also have PTSD issues. And technically, he didn't exactly threaten her. He just grabbed hold of her arm." From what Jake had told him, her jacket, but that was close enough to put the guy smack in the middle of Mike's sights.

"Which would have been enough to trigger possible PTSD issues of her own," Eleanor murmured.

He shot her a look. "Now who's the investigator?"

"You're an investigator. I'm a volunteer researcher. Though, in some respects, I suppose there's not a lot of difference," she said mildly. "I Googled both of you while you were off having coffee. The kidnapping must have been a horrible time for you."

"It wasn't a cakewalk." He brushed it off as he tended to do whenever the topic came up, then decided, for some reason he'd think about later, to come clean. "It was hell." He decided this was too early to mention how it had also caused a slow, painful death to his marriage.

"Worse because you weren't only her father but a detective. One who had a reputation for closing more cases, and more quickly, than anyone else on the force."

"You're not only thorough, you're quick." He and Tess hadn't been in the cafe that long.

"Not always." Despite the serious turn the conversation had taken, she gave him an up-through-the-lashes look.

"Quick can be a good thing. But there are also times I prefer things slow."

The pheromones were bouncing around like metal balls in a pinball machine inside the car as he pulled into her driveway. Suggesting that sometimes fate was generous, she'd taken advantage of Portland's public transportation system to get to work this morning, so they hadn't had to deal with two cars.

Her eyes, gleaming in the dashboard lights, were like emerald pools. As he felt himself drowning in them, Mike didn't have a single desire to be rescued.

"You're not talking about Googling or investigations anymore, are you?"

"I can see why you were awarded all those citations," she said on a purr. "Because you've definitely caught me, detective."

The hand that had checked out his biceps splayed across his chest. "You know what they say about life being too short. Fortunately, nights can be long."

As she led him by the hand into the house, and without a bit of social foreplay, like drinks or chit-chat, up the stairs to her bedroom, Mike decided that she only had that half right. Because the way he saw it, they'd caught each other.

26

SOMETIME IN THE early morning, Tess heard the water running in the downstairs bathroom and realized Nate was taking a shower. And wasn't that thought enough to trigger a flash of hormonal lust?

By the time she got through her own shower, dried her hair with the diffuser, and got dressed, the rich aroma of coffee was drifting up the stairs. Apparently he'd not merely invaded her life but her kitchen, as well.

In the cold light of day Tess wondered why on earth she had allowed Nate to stay in the first place. After all, her house was well secured—there were locks on all the windows and double bolts on both the doors. Her caller wouldn't have been able to get in even if he wanted to.

For the sake of argument, Tess chose to ignore the fact that no lock would be able to keep out an individual determined to gain entrance. She preferred to concentrate on all the reasons she was going to throw Nate Breslin out of her house the minute she went downstairs.

Work. That's how she was going to spend her day. Preparing for the Vasilyev hearing and Schiff trial.

As she went through the living room, she noticed that he'd folded his sheets and blanket and put them on the end of the couch with the pillow squarely on top. Wondering if he'd learned that at Marine boot camp, she continued into the kitchen, only to find that he wasn't alone.

"What are you doing out of the hospital?" she asked Donovan.

"Strategizing," he said easily. He was sitting on the barstool, crutches beside him. The hand that wasn't wrapped in fresh white gauze lifted a mug in greeting. "Good morning to you, too."

"I can't believe they let you out so soon." A thought occurred to her. "You didn't drive here, did you?"

"No, although legally I could have, since my left leg has the fracture, I hitched a ride from a patrol cop. As for getting out this morning, there wasn't any reason to keep me. If they hadn't been afraid of swelling from the concussion, they would've sprung me from the ER as soon as the doctor put the cast on my leg."

"You should at least be home. In bed."

There was a sudden suggestive glint in his eyes that told her he'd immediately thought of a too-easy, snappy comeback to that, but, with the Marine standing on the other side of the island, thankfully kept it to himself.

"Why don't you have some coffee?" Nate entered into the conversation, holding out another mug toward her. "Before you pack."

"Pack?"

Donovan looked as surprised as Tess was. "You haven't told her?"

"Told me what?"

Nate didn't immediately respond, first directing his answer to the detective. "I'd planned to fill her in on it when she came down for breakfast."

"*She* just happens to be right here in the kitchen." Tess positioned herself between the two men. "Fill me in on what?"

"Maybe you'd better tell her," Nate said to Donovan. "She seems to take orders better from you."

"I don't take orders from anyone!"

"I don't know." Donovan eyed Tess as if she were a powder keg about to explode. "I've never seen her so close to losing her temper before."

"It's probably just the stress," Nate suggested.

"Perhaps," Donovan allowed.

"If one of you doesn't tell me what you have up your sleeves right now, you're going to see an explosion that will make Mount St. Helens' eruption seem tame by comparison," Tess warned.

"See what I mean?" Donovan said to Nate. "Okay, okay," he said, turning back to Tess. "You're going to spend the next ten days at Shelter Bay."

"I'm what?"

"Just until the Russian mobster's hearing," Nate added.

Tess threw herself defiantly onto a barstool. And took a long drink of coffee, which, dammit, was better than she made.

"I'm not going anywhere with you," she said. "As for you, Donovan Quinn, how could you have forgotten that the Schiff trial starts Monday? You investigated that case. You're due to testify."

"You've gotten a continuance from Judge Lawson," the detective said with a reassuring smile. "So, you see, there's nothing to stop you from going to the coast with Breslin."

"Except for the small fact that I don't remember asking for a continuance."

"Tom got it this morning. After I told him about your latest phone call. And the slashed tire."

"Tom? As in Thomas Barnes? My boss?" The fact that the district attorney would pull rank on her, going behind her back to get a continuance on a case she had slaved on for months, was even more irritating than their plan to hide her out in Shelter Bay.

"Someone had to. And I had a hunch you would have refused to request the time."

"You're right. I would have. But continuance or not, I'm still not leaving town."

"You don't have a lot of choice," Donovan informed her, reminding Tess of her father when he put his foot down. Cops.

"The Vasilyev family's undergoing a lot of internal strife with the boss on the inside," Donovan said. "It's not just your snitch who's willing to share information. More than one member has come to us, volunteering to talk just to get others in the gang put away. It's imperative that we keep the boss from getting out of prison to smooth things over."

"Keeping him in prison is exactly what I intend to do," Tess reminded him.

"And you will. Thanks to Judge Conklin's helpful pen, Tom managed to get a continuance on the appeal, too," Donovan said. "So you can either spend the next ten days in a hotel room with a couple of uniforms guarding you around the clock or go down the coast and take some R and R in Shelter Bay. Breslin's house is remote enough that you should be safe until the hearing."

"And of course I'll be there to protect you. Day and night." Nate's wicked grin didn't make Tess feel very safe at all. He was hot when he grinned. And worse yet, he knew it.

She didn't want to go to Shelter Bay.

But she knew all too well that she would never be able to stand being essentially kept prisoner in a hotel room for ten long days. And even longer nights. Ever since her abduction she'd had a deep-seated aversion to being confined in even the most spacious hotel room. Tess knew it was silly—over the years she'd attempted various types of behavioral therapy, even resorting to hypnosis, to no avail. Nothing had ever worked.

"What about my caseload? I can't just run off and leave all my other cases in limbo."

"You're well covered. You've currently only got a couple B and Es that shouldn't even take a day each, and you've pretty much already set up the chop shop case for the guy to deal. So Tom assigned Mitchell to them."

That news did nothing to lift her spirits since Tess had always felt that if there were corners to be cut, Bill "The Slug" Mitchell would find them. Unfortunately, it didn't appear she was going to be given much of a choice.

"Does Dad know about this?"

"It was his idea."

"When did you two…" Comprehension dawned. "You and he came up with it when he was in talking to you last night." She turned toward Nate. "Then, while I was talking to this guy, you were brought into the plan."

"I couldn't exactly refuse when your dad dealt me in," he said.

"You do realize that if you don't accept some bodyguards, Mike will stake out your place, watching for intruders," Donovan said.

Tess knew how those long-drawn-out hours of surveillance spent drinking too strong coffee and eating junk food for hours on end could take a toll on men a great deal younger than Mike Brown. She wasn't prepared to risk her father's health for any reason.

"You know I wouldn't want that."

"Okay." Donovan rubbed his hands together as if he hadn't expected any other outcome. Which he hadn't. A good detective could always create corners to box a person into. Tess just wasn't accustomed to being on that end of the situation. "Now that we've got that settled, I'd better get going."

"I'll walk you to the door," Tess said, ignoring Nate, who wisely kept his mouth shut and stayed where he was.

"Nate's a great guy, Tess," Donovan said as they stood together in the foyer. "And he seems to care a lot about you."

The question was more than evident in his tone. "He may be researching a book on my great-great-grandfather."

Donovan examined her face. "Maybe. Maybe not. But it's obvious that he's a hell of a lot more interested in you than any one of your ancestors."

"Maybe," she admitted. "But there happen to be extenuating circumstances that you wouldn't believe if I told you."

"I'd believe anything you told me," he argued. "Didn't I accept your word that we could never be anything but friends?"

"You agreed," she corrected. Surely he hadn't been carrying a torch all this time?

"I did. Though, at the time, it wasn't my first choice, you were right. And before you start feeling guilty about dumping me—"

"I did not dump you!" Momentarily forgetting about his injuries and the fact that the man was, after all, on crutches, she slapped his upper arm.

Just as Nate obviously knew his grin was hot, Donovan knew his was cute. And had never been above using it when it served his purpose. "You're right. No one dumped anyone. Let's just say that we came to the mutual, adult decision that sex, as stupendous as it would've been, could risk screwing up a good thing we had and, I like to think, still have going."

He bent his head, brushing his lips against hers. "Take care, babe. I'll do my best to catch your caller."

Tess watched him go down the steps and to the waiting patrol car parked in front of her house, then returned to the kitchen, where Nate was waiting.

"Well, if I'm going to be held prisoner in Shelter Bay, I may as well get packed," she said, sounding cranky even to her own ears. The man didn't deserve her testy mood. If they were going to survive the next ten days locked up together, she was going to have to work on her attitude.

27

"I LOVE THIS DRIVE," she murmured an hour later as they drove through the fog- shrouded mountains from Portland to the coast. It had begun to rain, creating an intimacy inside the car as the tires hugged the roads on the twisting switchbacks. An intimacy that encouraged conversation.

"I know what you mean," Nate said with a smile. "I'm glad you're finally willing to talk to me. I was afraid I was going to be given the silent treatment for the next ten days."

"I wasn't giving you the silent treatment."

"Weren't you?" He only took his eyes from the winding road for a moment, but the brief glance was enough for Tess to read the challenge in his gaze.

"All right, perhaps I was. A bit. But you were incredibly high-handed back there," she insisted, jerking her head back in the direction of Portland.

"It probably came off that way," he allowed. "But in defense, after listening to arguments from guys who know what they're talking about and obviously care for you, it seemed like the best plan."

"My mother tried to escape the curse," Tess offered, breaking the silence that had settled over them. Having already decided, while she'd been packing, to try to concentrate on the positive, she liked that Nate seemed comfortable with silence. She wondered if it had something to do with spending so many hours working alone.

"By running away?" he asked.

"No. That came later. In the beginning, she wasn't anything like the woman she appears to be now. I've given it a lot of thought over the years and came to the realization that she decided that, curse or not, part of the reason her grandmother's and mother's love lives had failed was that they'd put their own needs and social causes first.

"Which is why, I suspect, Mom married my dad. It was obvious, when she still lived with us, that they were in love. Even as a child, I could sense their connection, their chemistry, without fully understanding it."

"Opposites attract."

"True." And wasn't that what Alexis had said about her and Nate? "I think, being a cop, Dad represented stability and strength, something my mother hadn't known a lot of growing up."

"How did they meet?"

"He was a PPB patrolman at the time. He stopped her for speeding through Lauralhurst. She was late to a meeting with a realtor." Tess surprised herself by laughing at a personal memory. "She was never on time to anything. But while it might have driven other more punctual people crazy, she always claimed that Italian time was different, more leisurely, than U.S. time."

"Having spent a memorable R and R in Italy, I have to agree with her," Nate said. "And there's admittedly something to be said for living life at a slower pace...So, he gave her a ticket?"

"No." Tess smiled at the memory of the story she'd always loved. One that seemed to have happened in a different lifetime. Because, she thought, it had. Hadn't her entire life been divided into *before the kidnapping* and *after the kidnapping?*

"He wrote her a warning. And told her to keep it on the dashboard so she'd remember that speeding was dangerous. And that he'd hate for her to get into an accident."

"And that was that. Here was this hot guy, wearing a uniform, who cared about her," Nate guessed.

"Because she grew up with a succession of housekeepers, while my grandmother traveled for various causes, she wasn't used to being treated as someone worth caring about," Tess confirmed.

So, Nate Breslin was not only polite, neat, talented, and, his Marine service would indicate, patriotic and loyal. Along with being pretty damn hot himself, he was also perceptive. The man was racking up more and more points. Which invited the question of why she was even fighting her attraction.

"She said she fell right then and there," Tess continued. "Apparently it was mutual, but because they came from different worlds, and he wasn't one of those cops who used his badge to hit on women, he reluctantly let her get away."

"Which meant she made the first move."

"She did. Dressed in a scarlet-as-sin red dress she bought that same afternoon, she showed up the next day at the police station with a plate of homemade cannoli."

"A beautiful woman in a red dress bearing Italian pastries and intent on seduction would be pretty damn irresistible."

Although it caused a little tinge of regret, knowing how the marriage had turned out, Tess laughed and was glad that her parents had some good years together before everything had come crashing down on them.

"They were engaged two weeks later and Dad moved into the house she'd been on her way to look at. The bungalow he still lives in. They married in the vineyards that summer while the dark purple Pinot Noir grapes hung heavy on the vines. She told him that it was a sign that they'd have many children."

"Why have many when one's so perfect?"

"Again with the writer words," she tossed back at him.

"Those just happen to be absolutely true."

Despite having always had her dad's love and support, Tess realized, for the first time, how her mother must have felt when, during that traffic stop, Portland Police Officer Michael Xavier Brown had made her feel valued.

"Those were good years," she said softly. Despite how everything had turned out, the memories warmed her heart. "Having determined not to follow in the footsteps of the other Lombardi women who'd come before her, my mother centered her life around her family. Looking back on it, some might consider her the Italian version of a Stepford Wife. She was always in the kitchen, and when she wasn't cooking, she worked overtime to make our home warm and welcoming. She even taught herself to sew so she could make my Cinderella Disney Princess bedroom curtains and bedspread.

"She restored pieces of antique furniture she unearthed stored away in an old barn at the winery, and people driving through the neighborhood would actually stop to take pictures of the front gardens. She had a definite talent for design."

Another lost memory came flooding back—a memory of her mother going out in the misty mornings with a wicker basket and scissors and humming happily as she deadheaded the roses.

"Sounds as if she was a true homebody."

"She was. Going against tradition worked for her. She'd found her calling. and those were wonderful years. I always knew my parents loved each other. And that I was loved. And safe."

Until she wasn't.

"After what happened...it was as if the kidnapper hadn't just taken me. He'd stolen my mother's spirit. And her heart. She fell into a depression and spent most of her time in bed. And even when she would join us for meals or some required family event at the winery, she became a mere ghost of herself. And I can't remember ever seeing her smile again."

"I'm sorry."

"So was I. She did have therapy and medication. But nothing seemed to work. Then one morning, as Dad was packing my school lunch, she came downstairs, dressed to go out, her hair and makeup done for the first time in ages, and announced that she'd decided to go out and indulge in some retail therapy.

"I don't know how Dad felt, but I got on that school bus happy for the first time in a long while. Because I believed that just maybe things were going to go back to the way they'd been. I watched the clock all day, waiting for the school day to end so I could see what she'd bought. I even wondered if it would be like before, when she'd return from shopping with a new lamp for my bedroom, or a unicorn for my collection, or maybe she'd even bought me a new dress for my school picture the next week. When I got off the bus, I ran the half block home."

"And?" Nate reached across the console and took hold of her hand. Accepting the wordless comfort, Tess didn't pull hers away.

"The house was empty. I thought maybe that she'd been having such a good time, she'd stopped to have lunch. Maybe with a friend she'd run into. Then I saw the note on the kitchen table to Dad. And I knew."

The chill was back. And although she knew it was physically impossible, Tess could feel her heart plummet, the same way it had that day.

"I ran upstairs to my parents' room. She must have packed after I'd left for school, because most of her clothes were gone. She'd also taken her jewelry. Except her wedding ring. Which she'd left in the holder on the dresser."

"Hell. That must have been really tough. I'm sorry."

Tess shrugged even as her eyes filled. "Like you said, things change after a major event in a family."

"She couldn't take it," he said. "Probably the guilt she was feeling from not protecting you just weighed her down and eventually got the best of her. Did you ever think that perhaps she knew she was hurting you and your dad? So, she did the only thing she could think to do to make your lives better. Leave."

"To run off to Monte Carlo? And Paris? And Saint Barts?" Photos of Claudia Lombardi, lounging on various gleaming white yachts, wearing a skimpy bikini, and holding up a martini glass, had been a supermarket tabloid front cover staple year after year. It had gotten so that once winter came to the States, Tess hated going grocery shopping.

"It's probably easier not to think when you never stay still," he suggested. As an oncoming car crossed the line on a particularly tight switchback, he returned both hands to the wheel. And left her missing his touch.

"Western monarchs manage to fly all the way from Northern Canada as far as Baja, California, but no one ever thinks of them as having amazing stamina," he said. "They just see them as beautiful butterflies flitting from flower to flower."

"Acting solely on instinct," she murmured. "Without any complicated thought process about the distance they have to travel, how many generations it'll take to make the journey, or all the dangers they'll face along the way."

"In those moments, they're just in it for the nectar," he agreed.

Tess thought about that as the sea came into view. "That's a very good analysis of a woman you've never met."

"I'm a writer. I spend a lot of time and thought delving into the motivations of my characters. Living in their skins, thinking their thoughts. Feeling what they feel. Your mother isn't all that different than many others who've suffered profound emotional pain. It's just that her name and money, along with your kidnapping, get her more attention than most and make her appear to be nothing but a shallow, narcissistic heiress. Yet, from what you said about your early years, she's anything but."

And didn't that have Tess realizing that one of the things that had always bothered her about the grainy tabloid photos was the way, while her mother's red lips would be smiling, her eyes would be flat. As if she'd checked out years ago. Which, in a way, she had.

For the first time, she realized that, in her own way, leaving had required strength. As much as the desertion had hurt, Tess couldn't imagine overcoming discovering that her mother had taken the easy way out with suicide.

Folding her arms, as if to hold in her own secret turmoiled emotions, she turned toward him, as much as the seatbelt would allow. "How would you write me?" Tess was genuinely curious.

"Ah," he said. "Good question. You'd be a challenge. Being that you're as complex as I suspect all the Lombardi women before you have been. You'd definitely be a heroine. Or more specifically, the hero of your own story."

"I like that," she admitted.

"Not that it's been an easy journey. I'd write you as a woman who, at too young an age, had her childhood and her innocence stolen from her. Through no fault of her own. Which hasn't prevented her from suffering from 'what if-itis.'"

How could he have nailed that so closely? Tess couldn't count the times over the years she'd wondered how her life would have turned out if she hadn't stopped and talked to that man in the van. If she hadn't accepted his offer of a ride back to her grandparents', which only made sense since the day had been hot, the road dusty, and, as he'd suggested, this way she could point out the way to the turnoff that would lead him back to the freeway.

What lives would her parents be living if she'd refused to talk to him and just kept walking? Even more ironic was that she'd always been a bookworm. Inspired by all those hours at the library, she'd fully intended to grow up and write her own stories that others could someday read. But because of that one split-second decision, her life had taken an entirely different path.

Tess had a career she was both good at and proud of. But she couldn't deny the irony that very same career was, in a very significant way, responsible for her being here, with a man who made his living with words. Who wrote the books other people read.

That led Tess to another thought…that the writing talent that had always won her gold stars on her school essays was partly responsible for her having the highest conviction rate among her peers. Because, just as Nate said he did while crafting his fiction, she always put herself into the skin of both the victims and the criminals. Studying them, learning them, she was able to share their stories with juries and hopefully make an emotional connection. Which, in turn, would lead to an informed decision.

"What else?" she asked.

"Let's see." Nate rubbed his jaw, as if pondering the matter. But his acting skills weren't as well-honed as hers. Although he was pretending to be speaking off the cuff, Tess could tell that he'd already given her a great deal of thought.

"Although she'd be intelligent and self-aware, that wouldn't stop her from carrying her own sense of guilt into adulthood. Because she can't overcome the possibility that her actions caused her mother to leave and break up what sounds like a strong, happy family. Sometimes it's easier to believe in the existence of an ancient curse."

"You're not talking about some fictional woman any longer," she complained.

He shot her a look. "I told you the line between fact and fiction tends to get blurry. I also see her as having spent her life trying to live up to her father's sacrifice. And feeling the need to be perfect so he won't leave, too."

"I've never, not once, worried that my father would abandon me," she insisted.

"The woman doesn't," he agreed. "But it's not always easy to escape your inner child."

"Now you're talking like a therapist. Not a novelist," she complained.

"Writing is a form of therapy," he said. "Because I've been there, Tess. Which is probably why I understand you better than you might think.

"What would you say to stopping for lunch?" he suggested, abruptly changing the topic as they approached a restaurant perched on a cliff. As they'd come out of the mountains, the sun had broken through the clouds, offering a dazzling view of gleaming silver sea.

Tess was curious at what he'd left unsaid, but reminded herself that unless her caller was captured while they were eating lunch, she had time to learn whatever Nate personal story was holding back.

28

"THIS REALLY IS stunning," Tess said after a Dungeness crab Louis salad at an oceanfront restaurant. Their window table afforded a panoramic view of the sea.

"You're not going to get any argument from me. Fortunately, my writing allows me to live anywhere. But this coast is, for me, one of the few places on earth where one can truly live the good life."

As she took a sip of the crisp Lombardi Sauvignon Blanc she'd been pleased to find on the menu, Tess thought about spending your life surrounded by such scenery, experiencing the open friendliness of the people, walking on the beach every morning before work. Though, from what Kara had said about Shelter Bay's crime rate, there probably wasn't enough business to keep that many prosecutors busy. So, while for her, the idea of living on the coast was more of an occasional fleeting fantasy, she could definitely see the appeal.

"The danger," she suggested, "would be in confusing life in such an elysian place with reality."

Nate didn't take his eyes from hers. "Is that what you think I've done?"

Relief was instant. "I was coming for you," she said, her eyes wide, dark pools of longing.

"Seems we're on the same wavelength again."

Unreasonably nervous, Tess licked her lips. "I do love you, Nate."

"And I love you. So where does that leave us?"

His words brought with them that now familiar blend of pain and pleasure. Tess shook her head, her heart in her throat. "I don't know."

In the courtroom, she was strong, resolute, incomparable. In bed, she was a seductive siren. But now, with her soulful dark eyes brimming with tears, Tess reminded Nate that she was also human. Which meant she was far more vulnerable than she first appeared.

He wrapped his arms around her. He rested his forehead against hers for a long, silent moment. "Promise to tell me when you do?"

Tess wrapped her arms around him and held on tight. "I promise."

For Nate, for now, it was enough.

37

MIKE, WHO'D BEEN celibate more years than he cared to count, had come to love waking up in Eleanor's bed. She was snuggled against him, her arm across his chest, her breath rising and falling in her sleep.

Her bedroom was, hands down, the most feminine room he'd ever been in. Soft rosy-pink curtains hung at the windows, a flowered comforter was spread on the bed, and a needlepoint rug of mint-green leaves covered the center of the wood floor. Small Oriental ceramic bowls shared tabletops with tall white candles in glass holders.

A collection of delicate boxes was arranged atop her dresser, while baskets of potpourri scattered around the room gave off a faint scent of flowers.

Mike had never claimed to have a designing eye. To him, throwing out a week's worth of newspapers and junk mail off the kitchen counter and scarred wooden coffee table before his weekly poker game with Jake and the guys was as close as he'd ever get to decorating. He occasionally wondered if he was responsible for Tess's stark apartment that didn't boast so much as a plant or a goldfish.

When he'd worried about that to Eleanor, she'd assured him that his daughter's working hours probably were the reason that she wasn't into as much clutter as she, herself was. Mike didn't consider the sexy librarian's decorating scheme cluttered. From that first night, when she'd coaxed him into sharing a bubblebath in the jetted tub that had left him smelling like flowers, he'd decided that the woman's romantic surroundings suited her to a T.

After having made love long into the night, they'd indulged themselves by sleeping late. But instead of a luxurious, slow awakening, he shot straight up, feeling as if someone had just shot a bullet into his brain.

"What's the matter?" Eleanor was instantly awake. "Are you all right, Michael? Do I need to call 911?"

"I'm fine." Although he felt as if someone had just walked over his grave. "I have to leave."

"So soon? Before you eat?"

Sitting in the plant-filled nook, watching her bustle around the kitchen making him breakfast had become a highlight to his days. Coming a close second to their lovemaking. Not today.

"I need to get to Shelter Bay. Tess is in trouble."

Mike didn't know how he knew. He just did. His instincts had never failed him. Except for that hellish time when he'd almost lost his daughter for good. He was not going to make that mistake again.

He was already out of bed, picking up his clothing that was scattered all over the room. They'd been to a supper club on the river the night before, listening to a Sinatra impersonator who hadn't been half bad. And apparently he wasn't the only one who liked Old Blue Eyes, because Eleanor had practically attacked him when they'd gotten back to her house.

"I'm coming with you."

"That's not necessary." Where the hell were his boxers?

"Here." She pulled them off a lamp covered in cream-colored silk. "Give me five minutes to shower and dress, and we'll be on the road."

While she was in the bathroom, he called Kara, who promised to get out to Sunset Point right away. Unfortunately, when he tried to call Tess, he kept getting a "no signal" response.

Despite his frustration at not being able to get hold of his daughter, Mike appreciated that Eleanor hadn't asked any questions about how he knew his daughter was in trouble. He also decided, as she came out of the bathroom already dressed, that he hadn't seen anyone take a quicker shower since his Marine days on an aircraft carrier.

"Whatever the problem is, you'll take care of it," she assured him as she climbed into the passenger seat and buckled her seatbelt. "And don't forget, she's got Nate Breslin with her."

As he tore away from the curb, headed west, Mike only hoped that the Marine would protect Tess. And that he'd get there in time.

38

THE STORM HAD the house in its grip; the thunder sounded like cannon fire as blue-white lightning flashed across the sky, arcing from black cloud to black cloud. Tess remembered how she'd thought Nate well suited to the rugged coast. The past days had only deepened her belief that he belonged in this fiercely dramatic country. As she belonged in her quirky, civilized river city.

Even as Tess reminded herself of that, she had to admit that Nate had a point. They were two adults. Surely, if they truly loved one another, they could find a compromise solution to such pedestrian problems as work and housing. A thunderclap crashed as fat raindrops spattered on the roof. Then there was a blinding flash of lightning, instantly followed by another shattering crack.

"Frightened?" Nate asked. He'd been running his fingers lazily through her love-tousled hair and couldn't miss the way she'd jumped.

Tess pressed herself more closely against him. "A little. You get some wild storms here."

He touched his lips to the top of her head. "None as wild as the ones we make ourselves."

She couldn't argue that. She was thinking perhaps that all she needed was to have him take her to bed or the outrageously decadent steam shower or Jacuzzi tub to help release the excess energy when her phone rang. Surprisingly, a familiar name appeared on the screen.

"Eric?"

"It's me," Eric Jensen said.

"How did you know where to reach me?"

"Our fearless leader told me. You remember him, don't you? The district attorney? The guy who signs our paychecks?"

"Of course I remember." She put the call on the speaker, so Nate could hear, as well. "You don't have to be so sarcastic," she shot back.

His tone turned immediately conciliatory. "Hey, I'm sorry, Tess. It's just that while you've been playing house with that writer guy, Vasilyev's not only killed your snitch last night, he's done an end run around us."

"He killed my informant?"

"Well, his fingerprints weren't on the shiv found in the guy's throat. But yeah, there's nobody around here or the prison who doesn't think he set up the hit."

"Damn." Her mind was spinning with what to do next when her colleague dropped a second bombshell.

"Even worse, he could be getting out of prison. Today."

Her fingers tightened on the phone. "What? How? His hearing isn't for another two days."

"His lawyer got his case slipped onto today's agenda. A guy with connections like that probably paid off someone. Maybe even a judge. The hearing's scheduled for two thirty."

Tess glanced over at the clock on Nate's bedside table. "But that's only—"

"Three and a half hours from now," Eric confirmed grimly. "But I think we can make it. I'm already in Shelter Bay with a trooper. We'll be there any minute."

That was a surprise. "But if you knew about the change in schedule, why did you wait so long to call me?"

"Everything's chaos around here. You were supposed to have been notified, but that must've fallen through the cracks. Everyone, from the D.A. on down, has been scrambling to find some legal precedent to block Vasilyev's latest move."

She heard him say something to whom she assumed to be the trooper. Probably giving directions, she thought. Located on the most westernly outcropping on this central part of the coast, Sunset Point wasn't the easiest place to find.

"We'll be there in five, at the most, ten minutes, Tess. Damn, I've got another call from Portland. See you in a bit." He abruptly ended her call.

"It's strange that they'd move the hearing without notice," she told Nate after she retrieved the suit and blouse she'd brought with her. After these days in casual clothes, it felt strange putting on what she'd come to realize was a uniform, not that different from the one Nate had worn during his Marine days. "Even stranger that Eric would come all the way down here, when it would save time to have you drive me back to Portland."

"Maybe now that your informant's dead, they want someone more official than me," Nate suggested, his eyes darkening as she shimmied into one of her standard charcoal pencil skirts.

"It's still odd about Eric. Though, thinking about it, he's had such rotten luck lately, maybe he just wanted in on the action."

"Could be. Too bad about your informant," Nate said. He'd surprised her by actually dragging a suit out of the back of his closet. It was odd seeing him out of jeans. Not bad, since it fit him as if it had been custom tailored, which it probably had been, and made him look like some titan of Wall Street. But she decided she preferred him in those fisherman sweaters he'd told her he bought by the dozen so he wouldn't have to make clothing decisions every day, and jeans.

"If Vasilyev didn't kill him, someone would probably have gotten around to it," she said. "If the people in prison played well with others, they wouldn't be in prison in the first place."

"I had a choice, when I started writing," Nate said. "I couldn't decide if I wanted to write thrillers or horror. Watching you makes me glad I chose what I did. I'll take living with ghosts and ghouls over stone-cold killers any day."

"It's probably tougher on cops," Tess said. "I come in later, after the havoc's been done. My job is to get justice for victims, which, while it has me dealing with the same type of people, at least has a positive goal."

"I suppose so. Aren't hearing schedules set months in advance?"

"The judicial board isn't known for such unpredictable moves. But Vasilyev's attorney has always been a slick operator. And, like Eric said, he could have bribed someone on the board to juggle the schedule in order to keep me from appearing."

"Which means whoever that was knew you were out of town."

"Good point."

And one she hadn't thought of. As Tess slipped on a pair of black suede pumps, she vowed to begin investigating the change in schedule as soon as she'd succeeded in blocking Vasilyev's latest attempt to make an end run around the system and get back out on the street. Maybe she could even hire her dad and Jake to look into it.

A dark blue Crown Vic with yellow stripes and the Oregon State Police shield on the door pulled up in front of Nate's house. A moment later, two men, one clad in a raincoat, the other in the blue uniform and silver badge of the Oregon State Police, were at the door.

"No offense," Nate said. "But we'd like to see your ID."

"I work with Eric," Tess said.

"No problem," the trooper, who hadn't taken off his blue campaign hat said easily. He pulled a business card with a photo ID, name, rank, and badge number out of his pocket.

"You look familiar," Tess said, studying the card after Nate had examined it. She handed it back and studied him more closely. "Have we worked together?"

"Not that I know, ma'am," he said politely.

"Are you ready to go?" Eric said. Despite the rain, he was sweating. Which showed, Tess thought, how nervous he was about this situation. With his track record of so many losses the past few months, he couldn't afford to be involved with Vasilyev getting back out on the street.

"I'll be going with Ms. Lombardi," Nate said.

"I'm sorry, Mr. Breslin," Eric said. "But I haven't been given authority—"

"I said, I'm going with her." Nate's tone did not invite discussion.

"Oh, hell," the trooper said. "I knew this wasn't going to work." An instant later, he pulled out an S&W pistol and, to Tess's horror, shot Nate in the chest.

Nate staggered back, falling to the floor. But not before staggering into the massive stone entry table. Tess knew that, however long she managed to live, she'd remember the sound of his head hitting the edge before he crumpled to the ground.

"Oh, my God! Nate!" Tess dropped to her knees beside him, running her hands over his chest, his head, his face, which had blood pouring profusely down it from the wound in his head. Even as she said his name, over and over, he remained terrifyingly unresponsive.

"We've got to get out of here," Eric Jensen said.

"In a minute. We need the money shot." The trooper stood over Nate, lifted the ugly black pistol, and shot him one more time in the chest. Nate's body bucked. But unlike in the movies or TV, he didn't jump up, rip open his shirt to reveal his bulletproof vest, and single-handedly beat the bad guys to a pulp.

"Are you going to shoot me, too?" Tess asked.

"Now, wouldn't that be too easy?" the trooper said. "And too quick. Since we never got to finish our time together."

He flashed her a grin that went straight to her brain, and shattered whatever bubble her memory had been protected in. She'd seen that evil smile before. Whenever he'd enter her prison, carrying a bag smelling of fast food, and cheerfully greet her with "Hi, honey. I'm home."

Before she could fight or run, he pulled out a Taser. A moment later, there was a zapping sound, and Tess felt herself go stiff as a board and lose all motor skills. The strangest thing, was, that although she was as limp as overcooked spaghetti, she was totally cognizant as her kidnapper threw her over his shoulder, carried her out to the car, tossed her into the trunk, and slammed the lid.

Leaving her imprisoned in the dark.

Alone.

And, she feared, about to die.

39

NOT WANTING TO waste energy she'd need to escape when Eric and her kidnapper got to wherever it was they were taking her, Tess had to bite her lip to keep from screaming.

She didn't think she'd ever forget the sight of Nate, lying on that floor, two bullet holes in the front of the unfamiliar white dress shirt, and blood streaming down his handsome face. Tears were streaming down her face when the air in the trunk suddenly dropped at least twenty degrees.

"Blast it all, girl," the captain's deep voice boomed. "What mischief have you gotten yourself into now?"

"Unlike your damn curse that got you stuck between realms, my problem wasn't of my own doing." Tess was cold, tired, frightened, and in no mood to be polite. "Is Nate alive?"

"Aye, thanks to those bulletproof vests he got for both of you to wear. Although his ribs will be sore for a time."

"He was lucky the pistol wasn't high-caliber," she said. When Kara, yet again taking her job of protecting Shelter Bay residents seriously, had shown up at the house with the vests the first day, Tess had believed she and Nate were being overly protective. Obviously not.

What terrified her was his head injury.

"He also needs some stitches in that head gash from the table," MacGrath answered the question Tess hadn't yet asked. "But the damn fool refused to take time to have them done and insisted the sheriff just wrap it. He's out with the search team looking for you."

"You need to tell him where I am. Actually, *I* need to know where I am."

"You're headed along the coast road. I heard the scallywags talking about taking you to the cave."

"What cave?"

"It's one carved into the side of the cliff. Pirates hid their treasures there. My guess is that they intend to leave you there to drown."

A dark, rocky cave. Rising water. A slow death. That's what her kidnapper had planned. With a knowledge of evil that she hadn't possessed as a child, Tess realized that he'd never intended to let her go twenty years ago. Even after her mother had paid the ransom. He'd just been playing with them all for his own sick, twisted enjoyment.

"You need to untie me," she said.

"I wish I could, lass. But I can't."

"You're a sailor and you can't untie a simple knot?" she asked incredulously.

"I was a seaman," he corrected firmly. "A sailor's a blasted landlubber's term. And I'll have you know that there wasn't a man on any sea who knew his ropes better than Captain Angus MacGrath."

"You should be proud," Tess said dryly. "So let's see some seaworthy expertise."

"Hang it all, woman, in case you've forgotten, I'm dead. And those are earthly ropes."

Tess couldn't believe her ears. "Let me get this straight. You can walk through walls, you can rattle pots and pans, appear and disappear at will, but you can't untie a damn rope?"

"Aye. Unfortunately, that's the way the wind blows."

She couldn't take any more. When she began to cry noisily, the captain became openly distressed. "Now, now, belay that noisy female caterwauling."

"Why should I?" she asked between sobs. "I thought I saw the man I love die. I've been Tasered, tied up, locked in this trunk, never mind the fact that I happen to be claustrophobic, threatened, and I'm probably going to die at the very hands of the man who terrorized me when I was just a girl. Excuse me if I don't find haunting Nate's house with you an ideal way to spend eternity."

"You're not going to die. At least not yet. There's a whole crew of men out looking for you. Breslin and your father will save you."

"Dad's in Shelter Bay?"

"He just arrived. Seems he had a feeling something was wrong, so he came down here to rescue you."

"You somehow did that, didn't you?" Tess said. "The same as you put Isabella in Nate's dreams."

When the captain didn't answer, she realized this might be her only time to tell him what she knew. "Isabella never stopped loving you," she said. "And Lucia was your daughter."

"Why in the blue blazes didn't she tell me when I came to her?" he demanded. His normally booming voice trembled with what Tess realized was centuries-old emotion. "Why did she lie and tell me that the girl was her husband's? And that she'd never stoop to marrying the likes of me?"

"That was because she loved you. Enzo was a dangerously brutal man and she knew, that if you were to confront him, he'd kill you."

"She should have had more faith in me," he said.

"I suspect, by the time you returned from sea, she'd pretty much lost faith in anything and everyone. Except Lucia."

There was a long pause. Then, on a voice that might have been roughened by unshed tears choking his throat, he said, "Thank you, lass. For easing my mind. And my heart.

"Now, don't you fret." He'd gathered himself together and sounded like the bold, larger-than-life great-great-grandfather she'd amazingly come to know. "You'll be getting out of this mess soon enough."

As the temperature in the trunk warmed, ever so slightly, telling her that the captain was gone, Tess continued her silent prayers that Nate and the search party would reach her in time.

• • •

"DAMMIT, IT'S MY fault," Nate ground out. "I was supposed to keep her safe." If she died, it would be like Fallujah all over again. He'd already lost too many people he cared about to violence. But although there were still times when he suffered survivor guilt, Tess was different. As hard as having his battle buddies die in that battle had been, Nate didn't think he could survive losing the woman he loved. Wasn't sure he'd even want to.

"We'll find her," Mike said. The roughened stress in his voice suggested he didn't dare think otherwise. "I didn't raise a quitter. Tess isn't going to give up without one helluva fight. We're going to find Tess safe and sound. Then you can take over the worrying about her."

Nate only wished he could be as sure of that as her father was.

What Nate had no way of knowing was that Mike was torn between being sick with worry about his daughter and fighting the inner rage that made him want to kill her abductors with his bare hands.

It fucking wasn't fair. A man shouldn't have to go through this twice in one lifetime. When Tess had disappeared so many years ago, he had gone without sleep for weeks, obsessed with capturing her kidnappers. That time, being a PPB detective, when he'd located the former Lombardi housekeeper, he'd followed the letter of the law, had dutifully notified the New Mexico police, and arranged for her extradition to Oregon to stand trial.

Unfortunately, he'd gotten there too late and the housekeeper had been dead.

This time a very strong part of him hoped that he'd be the one to track the men who'd taken Tess. And then he'd kill them.

40

Finally, after what seemed forever, the car stopped and the trunk opened.

"There you are," the familiar singsong voice who'd been infiltrating her dreams more and more often lately said. "And didn't you turn out to be a beauty? I've thought about you over the years, you know. Followed your career. Watched you grow up. And waited."

"Why?" If she could keep him talking, the captain would bring Nate and her father and Kara here.

"Why did I wait? Because in the beginning, I stayed out of Oregon because I never knew what you'd remember. Later, I became busy with other girls. And occasionally women, as parents became more vigilant. Do you know how difficult it is to get a child to help you with directions?" he asked. "Or even find a puppy, which used to be a sure thing."

He shook his head. "I've no idea what the world's going to come to when such a cynical, distrustful generation grows up."

"Why now?" Keep him talking.

He shrugged. "Because you recognized me, of course."

"You looked familiar when you were at the door, but I never would have made the connection." Though, given more time, the way memories of the events had started breaking through, she might have.

"No. In the prison."

"What?"

"When you came to talk to the snitch you intended to use to bring down the Russian," he explained. "I was on the way to outtake to be released. I saw you pause and look at me. That's when I knew."

She vaguely remembered a guard and prisoner passing her in the hallways as she'd paused to collect her thoughts before going into the interview room. But she'd barely noticed him and certainly he hadn't triggered any memories. At least not consciously.

"You were in prison? For what?"

"That's not important." He waved her question away. "We don't have all day. The tide's going to start coming in soon." He untied her legs, which still felt wobbly, but left her hands restrained. "Start walking."

He held the gun to her side as the trio walked through the woods. The dark, damp earth had a yeasty smell, and what had seemed like a fairyland of ferns when she was walking through this same forest days ago with Nate was ominously threatening. The immense quiet of the shadowy rainforest closed in on her while the black, gesticulating trees seemed to reach for her. As a jay suddenly flew overhead, his screeching call echoing in the darkness, she had to bite back a scream.

"He stabbed a street hooker," Eric revealed.

"It was a very small knife," her kidnapper qualified. "And a very inept prostitute. She wasn't one of my special girls.

Just someone I used to let off a little steam. Unfortunately, she got away, and what I hadn't counted on was a security camera in that alley getting my license plate.

"However, proving that I'm smarter than your average cop, no one ever made the connection to my other diversions over the years. Such as those weeks you and I spent together."

Life meant nothing to him, Tess realized. He could kill her as easily as a normal human would swat a mosquito.

Still stalling, wondering how long it would take a ghost to reach Nate, she turned to Eric. "I don't understand. What do you have to do with Vasilyev?"

"I've been working for him for a while."

"Doing what?"

"Whatever he needs. Fixing juries, moving funds, letting him know about your snitch."

"You told him about my informant? So, essentially you had the guy murdered?"

"Prison's a dangerous place. Things happen. Especially when you get branded a stool pigeon."

"But why?"

Eric shrugged. "You know I like to play the horses. When I found myself into Vasilyev's mob for more than I could repay, he offered a way out. Luckily, since I just happened to be a deputy district attorney, I was more useful to him alive than dead."

Two thoughts hit at the same time. "Janet Kagan was laundering money for him. And you're the one who got to that jury member who held out and hung my trial."

"It wasn't that difficult. Turns out the soccer mom by day was a high-priced call girl at night. All I had to do was threaten to show her website to her minister husband." He snapped his fingers. "Problem solved."

"Your friend has been quite busy moonlighting," her kidnapper volunteered. "When word got out through the prison grapevine that he was doing work for the Russian, he became one of the most popular visitors at the prison. Which was why I hired him myself to keep an eye on you for me. Until I was released."

So much for having felt sorry for the guy. Although deputy district attorneys had to schedule visits, no one would have had any reason to cross-check inmates Jensen had been visiting with cases he was prosecuting.

"But you didn't succeed with the son's jury," she said to Eric.

"I didn't try. He's a big, strong kid. And not that bright. His mother ran that entire operation, just using him for muscle when needed. Vasilyev had a role for him as an enforcer. In fact, his first assignment was to take out your snitch." He actually sort of smiled at the irony. "Small world we move in, isn't it?"

Forcing herself to remain calm as she stumbled along with that ugly pistol digging into her side was one of the hardest things Tess had ever done. "You also killed Jim Stevens."

Her mentor who'd gotten Vasilyev convicted. She'd never believed that had been a boat accident.

"The Russian finds prison a drag. And he's a firm believer in sending a message. Stevens's death was part personal, part professional."

"So now you're going to kill me for him?"

"It isn't anything personal, Tess. In fact, I took a risk trying to scare you off with those calls when Vasilyev wanted you dead before the hearing. How was I supposed to know that you shared your old man's stubbornness?"

"My father will be in the front row at your execution."

"There's always that chance," Eric Jensen agreed easily. "There's also the chance that his heart will give out before he manages to figure things out."

"You bastard."

Jensen's shoulders lifted in another careless shrug. "It's either you or me, Tess. You can't blame me for wanting it to be you."

"He's right," her kidnapper rejoined the conversation as they came out of the clearing and she found herself walking toward the cliff. "The only thing he got wrong is that for the next few hours, you're far more valuable."

Taking the pistol from her side, he turned it toward Jensen and pulled the trigger. Once. Twice. A third time. Tess's former colleague had a look of stunned surprise on his face as he crumpled to the ground. Dead.

Inside, Tess was screaming. What no one watching her in court would ever know was that there had been a time when she'd suffered stage fright. By the time she'd graduated law school, compartmentalizing her feelings in a separate mental box had become second nature.

"Are you going to shoot me now?"

"As it happens, Vasilyev wants you to have plenty of time to understand exactly how badly you inconvenienced him."

"I'm not going to jump."

"Of course you're not," he said patiently. "You're going to walk very carefully, very slowly, down to the beach."

Tess wondered why, if he was going to kill her, he didn't just do it right here. Then she remembered what the captain had told her about the cave. And understood.

"Vasilyev's only part of the equation," he explained. "I never would have met Jensen if I hadn't ended up in the same cell block as him, so, since we were both after the same ends and he's not out yet, we agreed that I'd be the one to take care of you.

"Meanwhile, you and I never got to finish our party," he said, confirming her revelation. "So, I'm taking you somewhere private. Where it's nice and dry. At least it's nice and dry right now." An evil amusement gleamed in his eyes. "It'll be a different story when the tide comes in."

After whatever torture he found amusing, he was going to leave her stranded where she'd be certain to drown. But not right away. Not until she'd been sufficiently terror-stricken, scrambling atop rocks, struggling to stay out of the thundering, icy surf.

It was at that moment that Tess realized that Death did not wear a black hood and carry a scythe. In her case, he was clad in an Oregon State Police uniform and carried an S&W pistol. At the same time, crystal clear memories of her time in that dungeon came flashing back, like a DVR set on fast forward, and she decided that if she was going to die, it wouldn't be alone.

Tess knew her self-defense training hadn't prepared her to protect herself against an armed, stone-cold killer who appeared to have spent most of his prison time in the gym. But her pride, as well as her strong survival instinct, wouldn't let her go down without a fight. The worst that would happen is that she'd fall off the cliff. But she'd take him with her.

"You're remembering now," he said. One of the reasons they often got away with their crimes for so long was that sociopaths were good at reading people. Which was how they managed to draw in their victims.

She hoped this murderous sociopath only saw the memories. Not the plan.

"Did I mention you were always my favorite?" he asked rhetorically. "I couldn't stop thinking of you. For all these years, whenever I was with another girl, it was always you I saw."

When he ran the back of his hand down her cheek in an evil parody of a caress, she bit him. Only to be struck by a backhanded slap with the pistol that knocked her off her feet.

41

NATE HAD NEVER been as relieved to see anyone as he was the captain when the seaman suddenly called him away from the others to tell him Tess's whereabouts. Although it took a little convincing, since they weren't having any luck where they were looking, the search team decided to head toward the cliff leading down to the cave.

The problem was, Tess's captors had a good lead, and time wasn't in their favor. But having walked every inch of this coastline, Nate knew both the cliff and the cave well.

"Does the Shelter Bay sheriff's office happen to have a Remington 700?" he asked Kara. It was the civilian equivalent of the Marine MP40 sniper rifle he'd used when deployed.

"I've got something even better," Kara told him. "The military's been generous to police departments. I just happen to have an MP40."

She got it out of a locked case and handed it to him. It had been a few years, but some things you never forgot. "I'm also married to a former SEAL sniper who can spot for you."

Nate glanced over at Sax. "You up for this, frogman?"

"Absolutely, jarhead," Sax returned. "Let's go bring home your woman."

• • •

SAX DOUCHETT COULD not only cook like an Iron Chef, he was probably the best spotter Nate had ever worked with. With the captain guiding them (having hung out with his own ghosts, Sax wasn't freaked out by him the way some people might've been), they found a spot hidden in the trees five hundred yards from the edge of the cliff, where they could see the guy in the blue trooper uniform shoot the deputy district attorney. Unfortunately, unlike in Iraq or Afghanistan, while they provided a good hide, the trees also presented an obstacle. After coming up with the best angle, Sax calculated the distance, wind coming in off the sea, and weather conditions, which were starting to get dicey with the thickening fog rolling in.

Not that anything was going to prevent Nate from making the money shot. All he needed was for Tess or the guy to move. Just a fraction of an inch.

His heart leaped up into his throat as he watched her bite the hand that had dared touch her.

"Don't breathe," Sax, who'd been a damn good sniper in his day, murmured.

Falling back on training that had once been as natural as breathing, Nate slowed his heartbeat and held his breath.

A moment later, Tess went down.

And Nate pulled the trigger.

As they watched the kidnapper fall over the cliff into the sea, Sax let out his own breath.

"I always said that if you guys had the high tech stuff we SEALs do, you'd be the best in the business," he said. "Good job. One shot. One kill."

Just as they'd both been trained to do, Nate thought, as he lowered the rifle and went to fetch his woman.

42

"I WAS SO AFRAID I'd lost you," he whispered into her hair. His voice was husky, rough with emotion. As she ran her fingers wonderingly over his face, Tess thought she detected moisture on his cheeks that was unrelated to the mist.

"Never happen," she assured him, smiling tremulously. "Because you're stuck with me, Nate Breslin."

His arms tightened around her with a strength that nearly cut off her breath. "Does that mean what I think it does?"

She nestled into his embrace, deciding that she could quite easily spend the rest of her life in Nate's strong, capable arms. "It means," she said, her eyes filled with the brilliance of love, "that you and the captain are going to have to get used to a woman living at Sunset Point."

He bent his head, kissing her with a rough tenderness that almost managed to make her forget the trauma of the past few hours. "Let's get out of here and go home."

"Home," she agreed fervently.

•••

TESS WOKE SLOWLY, luxuriating in the feel of Nate's arms around her. It felt so good to be home after those two unbearably long days in the hospital. She'd tried to tell them that it was only a little concussion, certainly nothing to worry about. She'd fully expected Mike to put up a fuss and want her to be hospitalized, but when Nate had instantly sided with her father and the doctors, insisting that she remain in the narrow, lonely bed until all the appropriate tests could be done, Tess had known she'd met her match.

During the time she'd been missing, her father and Nate had become not merely friends, but allies, as well.

She stretched lazily, looking down into Nate's handsome face. As her gaze drifted down his body, she wondered if she would ever be able to look at this man without loving him. Wanting him.

In the spirit of compromise, they'd decided to spend Monday morning through Friday afternoon in Portland, then Friday night through the weekend, and holidays on Sunset Point. Tess understood that there would be times when Nate would require the inspiration provided by the rugged coastline for his work. During those times they'd simply have to work things out.

What was most important was their love. And as the captain had already demonstrated so clearly, where love flourished, anything was possible.

Deciding that making the man she loved breakfast in bed would be a romantic gesture—she was an intelligent woman, surely she could follow the instructions in one of Nate's many cookbooks—Tess crept carefully out of bed and slipped into a short satin robe.

As she passed the study, the letters on the computer screen caught her attention. Which was strange, because Nate hadn't written last night.